BOOKS BY ASHLEY BRYAN

The Adventures of Aku
The Dancing Granny
The Ox of the Wonderful Horns
Walk Together Children

BEAT THE STORY-DRUM, PUM-PUM

Beat the Story-Drum, Pum-Pum

RETOLD AND ILLUSTRATED BY

ASHLEY BRYAN

Atheneum ✱ New York

1980

LIBRARY OF CONGRESS CATALOGING IN PUBLICATION DATA
Main entry under title:
Beat the Story-Drum, Pum-Pum

CONTENTS: Hen and Frog.—The husband who counted the
spoonfuls. —Why Bush Cow and Elephant are bad friends. [etc.]
1. Tales, Nigerian. [1. Folklore—Nigeria] I. Bryan, Ashley.
PZ8.1.M8   398.2'09669 [E]   80-12045

Published simultaneously in Canada by
McClelland & Stewart, Ltd.
Printed by The Connecticut Printers, Inc., Hartford, Connecticut
Bound by A. Horowitz and Son/Bookbinders, Fairfield, New Jersey
Designed by Ashley Bryan and M. M. Ahern
First Edition

Hen and Frog

Hausa Tales and Traditions, vol. 1, translated and edited by Neil Skinner from *Tatsuniyoʻyi Na Hausa* by Frank Edgar. New York, Africana Publishing Corporation, 1969, pp. 141-142.

Why Bush Cow and Elephant Are Bad Friends

Folkstories from Southern Nigeria by Elphinstone Dayroll. London, 1910, pp. 72-75.

The Husband That Counted Spoonfuls

Hausa Tales and Tradition, vol. 1, translated and edited by Neil Skinner, from *Tatsuniyoyi Na Hausa* by Frank Edgar. New York, Africana Publishing Corporation, 1969, pp. 310-311.

Why Frog and Snake Never Play Together

In the Shadow of the Bush by P. Amaury Talbot. London, 1912, p. 386.

How Animals Got Their Tales

The Bavanda by Hugh A. Stayt. London, Oxford University Press, 1931, p. 349.

To the memory of my sister
EMERALD

Contents

Hen and Frog

I'VE TOLD ONE TALE, HERE'S ANOTHER
CALL YOUR SISTER, CALL YOUR BROTHER.

FROG AND HEN once met. They walked along together.
Hen strut two steps, pecked at a bug.
Frog bopped three hops, flicked his tongue at a fly.
Strut two steps, peck at a bug.
Bop three hops, flick at a fly.
Hen flapped her wings and spun around. Frog slapped his legs and tapped the ground.
"All in together now," clucked Hen.
"How do you like the weather now?" croaked Frog.

3

"O click clack," clucked Hen. "See that dark cloud? That's a sign, I know it. A storm's coming."

Strut two steps, peck at a bug.

"It's still a way far off," said Frog.

Bop three hops, flick at a fly.

"Good!" said Hen. "Then there's time. Frog, let's make a hut before the storm hits."

"A hut? Not me!" said Frog. "Here's a neat hole. I'm going to get into that. Uh-uh, I won't help you make a hut."

"Suit yourself," said Hen. "If you won't help me, then I'll make the hut myself."

Hen set to work and Frog jumped into the hole. While Hen worked, Frog sang:

"Kwee kwo kwa
Kwa kwo kwee
A hole in the ground
Is a hut to me."

Hen was a skillful hut builder. She flipped and she flapped, pieced, pecked and pulled every branch and straw into place. She put in two windows, a door, and thatched the roof, leaving a space in the middle for the smoke of the fireplace.

"Click, clack, cluck," she sang. "Click, clack, cluck, claa, clee."

The dark cloud came closer.

"Quick Frog," said Hen, "there's still time. Help me make a bed for the hut."

Frog sang:

"Kwee kwo kwa
 Kwa kwo kwee
 The ground in the hole
 Is a bed to me."

"Well!" said Hen. "If you won't help me then I'll make the bed myself."

So Hen built the bed all by herself. She lay down to test it.

"O click clack cluck," she sang, "click, clack, cluck, claa, clee."

The dark cloud came even closer.

"Frog," said Hen, "there's still a little time left before the storm hits. Help me gather corn."

Frog sang:

"Kwee kwo kwa
  kwa kwo kwee
  The bugs in the hole
  Are food to me."

"Uh-uh," said Hen. "If you won't help me, then I'll gather the corn myself."

So Hen gathered the corn all by herself. She piled it by the fireplace and then rolled some pumpkins onto the thatched roof. She ran into her hut and latched the door just as the storm broke.

"*Blam-bam-pa-lam! Blam-bam-pa-lam!*"

The thunder rolled, the earth shook, tree branches tossed, and Frog was jostled in his hole.

"Kwa kwee," he sang, "kwee kwaaa!"

The rain came down, it really poured. Hen went to the window and looked out. Frog was standing up in his hole, swaying and singing a riddle song:

"Her children dance madly
  Mama never dances
  Riddle me this, riddle me that,
  Riddle me 'round the answers.
  Mama is a tree trunk
  Her children are the branches."

"Fool," said Hen. "This is no time for riddles."

Frog stamped as he sang. Suddenly, *splish-splash*, what! Water rose in the hole.

"Eh, eh!" cried Frog. "What's happening?"

Slish-slosh, the water rose higher and higher, and Frog was flooded out of his home. He waved to Hen as he floated by her hut, and sang:

"All in together now
  How do you like the weather now?"

"Sing it!" said Hen. "But you'll soon croon another tune."

It wasn't long before the steady force of the rain stung Frog's tender skin, and he began to wail:

"Kwo kwa kwee
  Kwa kwee kwo
  The stinging rain is riddling me
  Where shall I go?"

Frog knew where he planned to go. He bounded for shelter. Hop, hop, hop, hop, hop, hop right up to Hen's hut.

"Hen, Hen!" he cried as he rapped on her door. "May I come into your hut?"

"No," said Hen. "Uh-uh! When I asked you to help me make a hut, you refused."

"If you don't let me come in," said Frog "I'll call Cat, the cat that eats little chickens."

"Go back to your hole!" said Hen.

"Cat! Cat!" yelled Frog. "Come and eat Hen."

"Shh" said Hen. She opened the door. "Hush your mouth! Shame on you, scamp! Come on in."

Frog hopped in and sat by the door. The rain beat down, but

Hen's hut was tight and the rain couldn't get in. Frog leaned against the door drumming his numb toes and rubbing his stinging skin. Hen sat by the fire.

"Hen" said Frog, "may I warm myself by the fire?"

"No," said Hen. "Uh-uh!

You didn't help me make the hut,

Hands on your hips.

You didn't help me gather wood,

Pursed your lips."

"If you don't let me sit by the fire," said Frog, "I'll call Cat, the cat that eats little chickens."

"That's not fair Frog, you wouldn't dare."

Frog opened the door and cried:

"Cat! Cat! Here's Hen Chick

Come and eat her! Quick, come quick!"

Hen slammed and bolted the door.

"Scamp!" she said. "You scim-scam-scamp! Go ahead then, sit by the fire."

Frog hopped beside Hen and warmed himself by the fire.

"Umm-umm," he said, "fire sure feels good."

Frog spread his tingling toes to the heat and stroked his skin. Hen busied herself roasting corn. Then she began to eat.

"Hen," said Frog, "may I have some corn?"

"No," said Hen. "Uh-uh!

You didn't help me make the hut,

Hands on your hips.

You didn't help me gather wood,

Pursed your lips.

You didn't help me pick the corn,

Rolled your eyes."

"Ah! so what," said Frog. "If you don't give me some corn to eat, then I'll call Cat, the cat that eats little chickens."

"And I'll call your bluff," said Hen.

Frog opened the window and called:

"Cat! Cat! Here's Hen Chick
  Come and eat her! Quick, come quick!"

Hen slammed and latched the window.

"Scamp!" she cried. "Greedy scamp! Here, help yourself."

Frog helped himself until all the corn was eaten. Then he rubbed his stomach, stretched himself and leaned back on his elbow. The food and the fire made Frog drowsy. He yawned.

"Hen," said Frog, "may I lie on your bed?"

"No!" said Hen. "Uh-uh!"

  You didn't help me make the hut,
  Hands on your hips.
  You didn't help me gather wood,
  Pursed your lips.
  You didn't help me pick the corn,
  Rolled your eyes.
  You didn't help me make the bed,
  An' it ain't your size!"

"If you don't let me lie on your bed," said Frog, "I'll call Cat, the cat that eats little chickens."

"Shh, shh!" said Hen.

Frog jumped up and down and bawled:

"Cat! Cat Here's Hen Chick
  Come and eat her! Quick, come quick!"

"Quiet, scamp!" said Hen "Lazy scamp! Go ahead then, lie on my bed."

Frog lay on Hen's bed and fell fast asleep. He was still snoring loudly when the rain stopped.

Hen stepped outdoors to see if the pumpkins were still on the roof. She kept an eye cocked for Cat.

"Well, all right!" she said. "Just where I left them."

She went in and slammed the door, *bligh!*

Frog sprang awake. The noise frightened him, and he dived under the bed.

"Come on out Frog," said Hen. "The storm's over."

Frog crawled out.

"I'm hungry," he said.

"Climb onto the roof and fetch us some pumpkins," said Hen. "I'll cook, and we'll eat."

"Umm," said Frog. "Umm, pumpkin. I love pumpkin." But he still just sat on the edge of the bed.

Hen looked out of the window. She saw a small dark cloud in the distance. She knew that sign well, uh-huh!

"Hop to it, Frog," she said. "You can rest while I'm cooking a pumpkin."

Frog went outside and climbed up onto the roof. He dislodged a pumpkin from the thatch and rolled it down. Hen stood by the window and watched the dark cloud approach. It came faster and faster and grew bigger and bigger and . . .

It was Hawk!

Hawk spied Frog rolling the pumpkins off the roof. Frog was too busy to notice anything, not even Hawk's shadow as Hawk hovered over the thatch.

Hawk closed his wings and fell swiftly, silently. Suddenly, *flump!* Hawk snatched Frog in his claws and took off.

"Help! Help!" cried Frog. "Hen help me, help! I'm being carried off."

"Eh, eh!" said Hen. "Why don't you call Cat? You know, the Cat that eats little chickens. Eh? Click, clack, cluck, claa, clee."

Hen watched the scene safely from her window. Hawk soared upwards.

"Good!" said Hen. "That's it. Take the little so-and-so away. I've had more than enough of him, little tough buttocks!"

Hawk flew higher and higher. If Frog did call Cat, Cat did not come.

So that was that. Hawk took Frog away, and Hen could relax again. She cooked the pumpkin and sat down to eat. She was so happy that she ate eighteen plates of pumpkin without a stop. Then she lay back on her little bed and sang:

"Click clack cluck
Click claa clee.
I ate pumpkin,
Pumpkin didn't eat me."

Why Bush Cow
and Elephant
Are Bad Friends

BEAT THE STORY-DRUM, *pum-pum!* Tell us a big story, *brum-brum!* The one about Elephant and Bush Cow, *thrum-thrum!* And of Monkey the messenger, *pittipong-pitti-pong!*

Bush Cow and Elephant were always bad friends. There was good reason why they didn't get along and could never settle their disputes.

14

Elephant was big, so was Bush Cow. They were nicknamed the Big Ones. They walked big, *brum-brum!* and talked big, *thrum-thrum!* It was the big, bad talk that got them into trouble, *pittipong-pittipong!*

Elephant liked to boast about his strength to everyone. He talked himself up and never missed making a slight or a put-down about Bush Cow's strength.

When Bush Cow heard that Elephant was bad-mouthing him, he felt ashamed and angry. He knew he was a good fighter and he feared no one. He told the tale-bearers a thing or two to take back to Elephant, *brum-brum!*

Wherever Bush Cow and Elephant walked, everyone stepped aside, no question about that. But because of the bad words that flew back and forth between them, neither Bush Cow nor Elephant would give way to the other. So whenever they met, they fought, *pum-pum!*

One day the Big Ones met on their way to market.

"Step aside and let me pass Bush Cow-ard," said Elephant, "or I'll braid your horns, *brum-brum!*"

"Out of my way, Snake Snout," said Bush Cow, "or I'll tie your trunk into knots, *thrum-thrum!*"

Greetings like that were bound to lead to blows. Elephant landed an opening clout; Bush Cow answered with a cuff; and then the bout was in full swing.

Bush Cow butted Elephant in his side. Elephant tripped Bush Cow with his trunk. They tumbled and tussled all over the field, pummeling each other as they rolled, *pum-pum! pum-pum!*

A crowd gathered. The village elders were distraught when they saw the torn-up field. They called out:

"Stop, stop! You're ruining the crop! Aie-yaie. It is as the proverb says: 'When two big ones fight, it is the grass that suffers.' Monkey, get closer and tell them to stop."

Monkey leaped into the tree nearest the fighters. He hung from the branches and chattered:

"Don't fee fa foo fight. It's not bee ba doo right."

Monkey's scat-talk was understood by everyone, but the Big Ones wouldn't listen to him. They kept on fighting.

Finally the Head Chief arrived and stopped the fight, for when the Head Chief commands, everyone obeys.

16

"What is happening here?" the Head Chief demanded.

Monkey hopped to him with his report:

"A fee fa foo fight. No bah ba dee body won. No nee na no noo, not one of the two. Not Bush Cow, I know. Not Elephant O. Wee why wo do they fight? What fee fa foo for? Their wee ba ree bop heads are hard as a door. It's always a draw."

"Door, draw!" said Elephant. "Suppose he hadn't stuck me with those horns, hah! I would have won, *thrum-thrum!*"

"Won, when!" said Bush Cow. "Suppose he hadn't tied my fists with his trunk, I would have flattened him, *brum-brum!*"

"Suppose, suppose," cried the Head Chief in disgust. "Suppose your head was a door post!"

Everyone laughed.

"But suppose," said the Big Ones, who were not laughing, "suppose we let you settle this dispute between us. We can't."

The Head Chief looked at the field and knew that something had to be done. He conferred with the village elders then announced the plan:

"Elephant and Bush Cow will meet to fight in the large open space of the marketplace next market day, *thrum-thrum!* This dispute will be settled then, once and for all, *brum-brum!* Everyone from country and town is invited to come and witness the battle, *pum-pum!*"

The Big Ones agreed, and all the details of the Battle of the Big Ones were settled. Then the villagers went on their way to the beat of the drums, *prum-prum, thrum-thrum, pum-pum, pittipong-pittipong!*

18

When market day of the fight dawned, Bush Cow rose early. He wanted to be the first one there to prove he was no coward. He limbered up quickly then lumbered along the main road. He heard that Elephant had not yet passed that way so he took up his position on the road to market at some distance from town.

Bush Cow blocked the road and waited. He became impatient and began bellowing and tearing up the ground, *brum-brum!*

"What have you done with Big Big One? Have you seen him? Where is he?" he cried to everyone who passed.

Monkey came along the road and was stopped and questioned.

"How should I na nee know of bee ba ba ray Big Big One?" said Monkey. "I'm a lee ba lu bay little monkey. But don't wa wu wait here. Sha ba dee boo no. Go on to the square. Chief a ree bop said oo soo bee doo fight there."

Bush Cow let Monkey pass, but he paid no attention to what he said. He stood right where he was. He stopped Doe, Zebra and Wild Boar with the same question before he heard Elephant trumpeting in the bush, *thrum-thrum!*

Elephant was breaking down trees and trampling the bushes in his way. That's how he kept in form for the fight. He came onto the main road to market. There stood Bush Cow, blocking the way.

"Move on to the square," said Elephant. "We agreed to fight there."

Bush Cow didn't like Elephant's tone of voice, so he stood his ground and glared at him.

"Move! Move Bush Cow-ard!" said Elephant.

"Move me then Snake Snout!" said Bush Cow.

"O me ma moo my," said Monkey. "Don't fee foo fight here. Move oo bee doo on to the square."

The Big Ones brushed Monkey aside. They didn't want to listen, and they didn't waste words. They lowered their heads and charged, *powf!* That was the end of their promise to fight in the marketplace.

A tremendous battle began. The Big Ones pitched, rolled and tossed, damaging the nearby farms. The villagers were frightened from going on to market and hid out of harm's way, hoping the havoc would soon halt. The village elders were shocked when they came on the scene. They couldn't believe the Big Ones would disobey the Head Chief's battle plan.

"Monkey," they said, "quick! Run and tell the Head Chief all that is happening here."

Monkey had watched the fight from the start so he knew the message. He set off quickly, swinging through the branches and squealing as he swung. When he stopped a moment to catch his breath, he could no longer remember why he was in such a hurry, where he was going and what he was to say to whom, which is the forgetful way that monkeys have.

"Now why, where, to who, what for?" he asked himself. "What, where, why, to who? Shoo bee do, shoo bee do!"

Monkey danced, "Hay baa ba ree bop, hay baa . . ." Suddenly the message sprang back into his mind.

"Skoo bee do, skoo bee do," he sang in delight. He went on as fast as he could go so that he would not forget the message again.

When Monkey reached the Head Chief's house he remembered, "Shoo bee do" and "skoo bee do," but nothing more. He hadn't the slightest idea why he had come.

Well, he had arrived and that was something. He could at least act as if he were about important business. Shoo bee do, shoo bee do! he'd look busy, yeah!

Monkey sat down and engaged in a minute personal inspection of his fur. A minute later whop! he jumped up onto the roof of the house, *pittipong-pittipong!* He caught and ate a bug, then down he swung again to the ground.

There he found a stone and he rolled it around, backward and forward, forward and back, in an aimless sort of way while looking in the opposite direction.

Monkey soon tired of this and picked up a stick. He tapped out a rhythm on the stone, *whick, whack-a-whack; whick, whack-a-crack!* the stick broke. He flung the pieces into the bushes and flung the stone after them.

Monkey hopped onto the verandah and crouched with his head in his hands. He was almost at wit's end when his attention was attracted by a large praying mantis that fluttered past him into the Head Chief's house. It circled the room with a loud clatter of wings then settled on the floor and immediately assumed its usual prayerful attitude.

Monkey stalked the mantis carefully and was just about to seize it when the chief caught sight of him and shouted out in a loud voice:

"Ha, Monkey, is that you?"

At the sound of the Head Chief's voice, Monkey did a back flip and mantis flapped out the front door.

"Who, who?" cried Monkey. "O ya you no me. Yes-siree, it's bee ba dee me."

"What brings you here?" asked the chief.

"To see shoo bee do you. Yeah!"

Monkey cocked his head to one side, trying to look as if he had something wise to add to that. Actually he was thinking of nothing. He began chattering nervously about sticks and stones and mantis bones because everything else had gone out of his head, *pittipong-pittipong!*

"Well" said the Head Chief "if you've nothing more on your mind than that, then help yourself to one of the ripe bananas hanging up in the verandah."

Monkey was very fond of bananas and didn't need to be told twice. He went quickly and chose a large one, then returned to the room. Monkey peeled the banana and bit first one end, then the other, as if that would make it last longer. He studied the banana carefully after each bite.

"Monkey," said the Head Chief, "shouldn't Bush Cow and Elephant be here by now? I've been waiting for them all morning. They promised to meet in the market square for the big battle today."

Yoweee! Monkey somersaulted and came down chattering: "O sure shoo bee do, sure, sure shoo bee do!"

Monkey swallowed the last bit of banana, and after all sorts of scat-talk, squeals and grimaces told the Head Chief all of the elder's message.

"Aha!" said the Head Chief, "so that's why the market is almost empty today. Thanks for the message, Monkey. Help yourself to another banana. As for Bush Cow and Elephant, I'll see to it that they get theirs, *thrum-thrum!*"

Monkey ate the banana, pleased and impressed with himself. He was sure that there were not many others who could manage a message to match his style, shoo bee do, shoo bee do!

The Head Chief called for his bow and arrows, and Monkey led him to the scene of the battle. When the Head Chief arrived and saw the ruined farmlands, he didn't ask questions and he didn't raise his voice. Instead, he raised his arm with the bow and shot first one arrow, then another, *plung, plung!*

Bush Cow felt a sharp stab in his rump, *wow!*

Elephant felt a sharp stab in his rump, *wow!*

The Head Chief didn't wait. He shot a second volley of arrows and prepared to shoot a third.

But Bush Cow and Elephant got the message. They didn't wait for any more arrows to fly. They flew! They plunged into the bush and disappeared, *brum-brum!*

After that the Head Chief refused to have anything more to do with settling disputes between Bush Cow and Elephant. But ever since then, when wild animals fight, they always fight in the bush and not on public roads, *thrum-thrum!*

Since the big battle between Bush Cow and Elephant was never decided, each still boasts that he is the stronger. Whenever they meet along main roads, they argue. Whenever they meet in the bush, they fight.

So to this day, *pum-pum!* Bush Cow and Elephant, *thrum-thrum!* remain bad friends, *brum-brum!*

Pittipong-pittipong!

The Husband
Who Counted
the Spoonfuls

ONCE THERE WAS a man named Tagwayi, as stubborn in his way as stone, but gentle as a leaf. He was a good man and good-looking, too. He had no trouble getting a wife, but he did have trouble keeping one.

Tagwayi couldn't stay married because he always counted the spoonfuls.

It wasn't only spoonfuls that Tagwayi counted. He counted everything he saw on his walks through the village and as he worked in his fields. He counted huts, people, chickens, trees and the rows he'd hoed in his field, all with equal enthusiasm. He loved the rhythm of counting and the sound of numbers.

Tagwayi counted for pleasure and not out of envy or greed.

The villagers admired Tagwayi's skill with numbers. He was often called in by the village elders to help resolve difficult number matters. But to count the spoonfuls of food served was considered a disgrace by all, as bad as knocking the spoonful of food out of another's mouth. No wife would stay married to a husband with such a rude habit.

Because of this, Tagwayi's first wife had left him, then the second and the third. Each time that Tagwayi married, he would manage to control his urge to count the spoonfuls for a week or two. Then he'd lose control and sing out the spoonfuls count.

"That does it!" the wife would say. "You did it! Good-bye!"

And the wife would go, leaving Tagwayi alone.

The villagers made up a song about him:

"He's a counting the spoonfuls, no'count,
  Can't keep a wife.
  A counting the spoonfuls, no'count,
  Hungry for life."

There was no telling how many wives Tagwayi had driven out with this stubborn habit. The villagers said: "More than you could shake a stick at!" As much as Tagwayi liked to count, he was too ashamed to keep count of his past wives. He'd had so many, and now he hadn't any.

He crouched in his hut by the burned pot of food he'd fixed. Rocking on his heels, he'd moan and lament for all to hear, but there was no wife there.

"Aie-yaie," he cried. "Here am I! What? Me one, all alone in this hut! Eh, eh? Don't I too need a wife?"

31

Tagwayi mumbled and muttered and talked crazy talk to the cooking pot, but talk didn't change the pot into a wife. Then he recalled the proverb: "The journey is on the road, it doesn't rest in the mouth."

Tagwayi stood up and counted his steps—one, two, three, four—that brought him to the door of his hut. Then five, six, seven, eight, nine, ten, eleven that got him across the compound. Twelve, thirteen, fourteen steps sped him on his way. Fifteen, sixteen, seventeen took him along the path that led to the villages beyond.

Tagwayi walked along kicking the spear-grass as he went. A hornbill alighted in a tree branch overhead and sang: "Chilin, chilin! chilin, chilin!" Tagwayi listened and counted the calls to feel the thrill of it all the more deeply. Ah! There was a good round count to the song. He was sure now that he would find a wife.

And he did, even though it meant traveling further than he'd ever traveled before.

"Today's a happy day," he sang. "I've found a wife."

"Chilin, chilin! Chilin, chilin!" echoed the hornbill.

Tagwayi couldn't wait to bring his wife to his compound. He took her hand.

"Let's go!" he said.

"Shouldn't we wait till morning? You might lose the way after dark."

"Oh no!" said Tagwayi. "I know the way, and later the moon will help us. Besides, it is said, 'Even in the dark, the hand that holds food does not lose its way to the mouth.' "

Tagwayi set out with his wife, and he had no trouble finding the way home by moonlight.

Now he was a happy man. Every morning, on his way to work in his fields, he made up a numbers song:

"Take two out of ten
 Split twelve for the four
 Add thirty threes
 To nine nineties
 Times six. Then halve the score."

The villagers heard him singing as he passed. They knew that although Tagwayi counted all the time, he sang his number songs only when he was very happy. He had a wife, she was a good cook and he ate well. They noticed a slight skip in his step as he kept time to the number tune.

When Tagwayi returned home from work in the fields, he watched his wife pound, winnow and wash the corn. He counted the number of times she repeated this until the corn flour was fine enough for the evening meal of tuwo. And when his wife poured the miya sauce over the tuwo he sang:

"The world's a pleasant place
 for two who eat tuwo."

"Chilin, chilin," sang the hornbill.

As his wife dished the tuwo into the calabashes Tagwayi asked; "What is the number for today?"

"What number foolishness is this you're asking about?"

"Uh-uh." Tagwayi laughed. "You won't catch me counting the spoonfuls. I've learned well that 'Whoever mounts the horse of Had-I-But-Known suffers trouble'!"

Tagwayi's wife spooned on, but it was a close call. After that he stepped outside whenever food was being dished out. He'd count trees, he'd count stones, he'd count butterflies and cries of the hornbill, "Chilin, chilin." And when he came in, he wasn't tempted to count at all, not one spoonful.

Two weeks passed, then three. One night Tagwayi circled the hut. He felt hungrier than ever, and he counted faster than ever, too. He counted himself out and was ready to enter too soon.

The hornbill alighted on the ground nearby and cried in warning: "Woh, woh! woh woh!"

Tagwayi said, "Woh, woh? No, no! Sing chilin, chilin!" But the hornbill sang, "Woh, woh!" again.

He didn't heed the warning and rushed into the hut. His wife had just begun to dish out the tuwo. Tagwayi squatted down beside her.

"One-a-spoonful, two-a-spoonful, three-a-spoonful, four," he began.

His wife was annoyed. She drew in her breath and sucked her teeth, "Choops." Tagwayi didn't notice a thing.

"Five, six, seven, eight, add a spoonful more."

"Choops, choops," choopsed his wife, but even her choopsing didn't get through to him. He couldn't stop counting.

"Nine spoonfuls, ten spoonfuls. Will not come again spoonfuls."

"And neither will I!" cried his wife. She klonked him on the head with the spoon and left.

The klonk brought Tagwayi back to his senses, but it was too late. His counting spoonfuls had driven out his wife again.

"Ah! This time I have fallen into the cooking pot," he said.

"Woh, woh! Woh, woh!" echoed the hornbill.

The next day Tagwayi walked around the village hoping to hear news that might lead him to a new wife. As he made the rounds, so did the song:

"He's a counting the spoonfuls, no'count,
   Can't keep a wife
   A counting the spoonfuls, no'count,
   Hungry for life."

Tagwayi was left with the days to count as they passed. His cooking didn't improve, and sometimes he burned the tuwo two or three nights in a row. Counting the spoonfuls hardly made up for that.

One day the hornbill sang again: "Chilin, chilin!" It was the day that Tagwayi heard about a woman who was the fairest in her town. He set off at once to her home to seek her in marriage.

"I have heard of you," she said.

"Oh," said Tagwayi. He knew what she must have heard. "Then you won't be my wife?"

"Chilin, chilin," sang the hornbill.

"We-ell," she said, "I'm not refusing you."

"You will then," he cried. "Oh, the world's once again a happy place!"

"Now listen Tagwayi so you won't have to mount the horse of Had-I-But-Known. If I marry you, there is one thing that will cause us to separate."

"Uh . . . er . . . what um . . . er . . . ah's that?"

"Your only failing is counting spoonfuls," she said. "Count sheep, count corn, count cowries. Count what you will, but in good health or ill, don't count spoonfuls!"

"Well," said Tagwayi, "if that's all there is to it, I promise I won't do it again. Since you say that is what you do not like, I'll see to it that I stay out of the cooking pot with you."

"Very well," she said.

So they were married, and Tagwayi brought his new wife to live in his compound.

The months passed. Every day Tagwayi went to work in his fields and sang his curious number songs. When he returned home, the hornbill sang in a tree outside the hut: "Chilin, chilin! Chilin, chilin!" The villagers no longer teased Tagwayi with their "Counting the spoonfuls, no'count" song. It seemed that at last he was well married.

During those months Tagwayi did as before. He counted outdoors until the meals were spooned into the calabashes. He kept to the proverb: "When the eye does not see, the heart does not grieve."

One day, as the hornbill sang, "Chilin, chilin!" Tagwayi hit on a new idea, a way to control his stubborn habit. He counted silently outdoors. After weeks of practice, he became so good at it that he no longer moved his lips. True, he did bat his eyelids and tap with a big toe for each count, but that was hardly noticeable.

Now he could sit indoors while his wife served the meals; his silent counting-the-spoonfuls system worked.

"Chilin, chilin!" sang the hornbill.

Tagwayi's wife was so pleased that he'd given up that stone-stubborn habit that she'd spoon in extra spoonfuls for him.

One evening Tagwayi sat on the edge of the bed, counting

spoonfuls silently as his wife spooned out the tuwo. He batted
his eyelids and tapped his toe to:

"One, two, in you go. Three, four and many more. Five, six
delicious licks. Seven eight . . ."

Just then a neighbor called from the entrance to the compound:

"Hey Tagwayi!"

"Nine!" answered Tagwayi.

His wife paid no attention, she didn't even say choops. She
just went on spooning out the tuwo.

Tagwayi talked with the caller, but he never took his eyes
off the pot. The hornbill flew down to the ground and warned,
"Woh, woh! Woh, woh!" but Tagwayi didn't hear.

His wife had reached eleven spoonfuls and was about to dish out the twelfth when Tagwayi came back in.

"If I hadn't told you that I had given up counting the spoonfuls," he said, "I should say that you have just put the twelfth spoonful into the calabash."

"You did it just now," she cried. "When you said 'nine,' I pretended not to hear, for I thought you had just forgotten. But no, you are back to your old rotten tricks."

"Old rotten tricks?" said Tagwayi. "Did you hear me count to twelve? Uh, it was twelve spoonfuls you dished out though, wasn't it?"

"Dished out, fished out!" cried his wife. "Now who's counting the spoonfuls?" She dropped the spoon on Tagwayi's big toe. "I'm not living with a husband who counts spoonfuls!"

The next morning his wife left.

"Count the grass!" she cried as she went, and she never returned to his compound.

"Woh, woh!" mourned the hornbill.

That was the last of the many wives that Tagwayi had. After that he never got another wife. He sat where his last wife left him and counted. And since it is the grass he counts, Tagwayi is counting still.

Why Frog and Snake
Never Play Together

MAMA FROG had a son. Mama Snake also had a son. One morning both children went out to play.

Mama Snake called after her child:

"Watch out for big things with sharp claws and teeth that gnaw. Don't lose your way in the bush, baby, and be back to the burrow before dark."

"Clawsangnaws," sang Snake as he went looping through the grass. "Beware of the Clawsangnaws."

Mama Frog called after her son:

"Watch out for things that peck or bite. Don't go into the bush alone, dear. Don't fight, and get home before night."

"Peckorbite," sang Frog as he went hopping from stone to stone. "Beware of the Peckorbite!"

Snake was singing his Clawsangnaws song, and Frog was singing of Peckorbites when they met along the way. They had never met before.

"Who are you?" asked Frog. "Are you a Peckorbite?" and he prepared to spring out of reach.

"Oh no! I'm Snake, called by my Mama 'Snakeson': I'm slick, lithe and slithery. Who are you? Are you a Clawsangnaws?" and he got ready to move, just in case.

"No no! I'm Frog, called by my Mama 'Frogchild.' I'm hip, quick and hoppy."

They stood and stared at each other, then they said together: "You don't look anything like me."

Their eyes brightened. They did not look alike, that's true, but some of their customs were alike. Both knew what to do when two say the same thing at the same time.

They clasped each other, closed their eyes and sang:

> *"You wish a wish*
> *I'll wish a wish, too;*
> *May your wish and my wish*
> *Both come true."*

Each made a wish then let go.

Just then a fly flew by, right past Frog's eyes. Flip! out went his tongue as he flicked in the fly.

A bug whizzed past snake's nose. Flash! Snake flicked out his tongue and caught the bug.

They looked in admiration at each other and smiled. The two new friends now knew something of what each other could do. They felt at ease with each other, like old friends.

"Let's play!" said Frog.

"Hey!" said Snake, "that was my wish. Let's play in the bush."

"The bush! In the bush!" cried Frog. "That was my wish. If you go with me, it's all right 'cause Mama said I shouldn't go alone."

Frog and Snake raced to the bush and started playing games.

"Watch this," said Frog. He crouched down and counted, "One a fly, two a fly, three a fly, four!"

He popped way up into the air, somersaulted and came down, whop!

"Can you do that Snake?"

Snake bounded for a nearby mound to try the Frog-Hop. He got to the top of the slope, stood on the tip of his tail and tossed himself into the air. Down he came, flop! a tangle of coils. He laughed and tried again.

Sometimes Snake and Frog jumped together and bumped in midair. No matter how hard they hit, it didn't hurt. They had fun.

Then Snake said, "Watch this!" He stretched out at the top of the mound and counted, "One a bug, two a bug, three a bug, four!" Then swoosh! he slithered down the slope on his stomach.

"Try that Frog. It's called the Snake-Slither."

Frog lay on his stomach and slipped down the hill. His arms and legs flailed about as he slithered. He turned over at the bottom of the slope, blump! and rolled up in a lump.

Frog and Snake slithered down together, entangling as they went. Their calls and laughter could be heard all over the bush. One game led to another. They were having such a good time that the day passed swiftly. By late afternoon there were not two better friends in all the bush.

The sun was going down when Snake remembered his promise to his mother.

"I promised to be home before dark," he said.

"Me too," said Frog. "Good-bye!"

44

They hugged. Snake was so happy that he'd found a real friend that he forgot himself and squeezed Frog very tightly. It felt good, very, very good.

"Ow! easy!" said Frog. "Not too tight."

"Oh, sorry," said Snake loosening his hug-hold. "My! but you sure feel good, good enough to eat."

At that they burst out laughing and hugged again, lightly this time.

"I like you," said Frog. "Bye, Snake."

"Bye, Frog. You're my best friend."

"Let's play again tomorrow," they said together.

Aha! they clasped and sang once again:

> *"You wish a wish*
> *I'll wish a wish, too;*
> *May your wish and my wish*
> *Both come true."*

Off they went, Snake hopping and Frog slithering all the way home.

When Frog reached home, he knocked his knock, and Mama Frog unlocked the rock door. She was startled to see her child come slithering in across the floor.

"Now what is this, eh?" she said. "Look at you, all covered with grass and dirt."

"It doesn't hurt," said Frog. "I had fun."

"Fun? Now what is this, eh? I can tell you haven't been playing in ponds or bogs with the good frogs. Where have you been all day? You look as if you've just come out of the bush."

"But I didn't go alone, Ma. I went with a good boy. He's my best friend."

"Best friend? Now what is this, eh?" said Mama Frog. "What good boy could that be, playing in the bush?"

"Look at this trick that he taught me, Ma," said Frogchild. He flopped on his stomach and wriggled across the floor, bungling up Mama Frog's neatly stitched lily-pad rug.

"That's no trick for a frog! Get up from there, child!" cried Mama Frog. "Now what is this, eh?" Look how you've balled up my rug. Just you tell me, who was this playmate?"

"His name is Snakeson, Mama."

"Snake, son! Did you say Snake, son?"

"Yes. What's the matter, Mama?"

Mama Frog trembled and turned a pale green. She sat down to keep from fainting. When she had recovered herself, she said:

"Listen Frogchild, listen carefully to what I have to say." She pulled her son close. "Snake comes from the Snake family. They are bad people. Keep away from them. You hear me, child?"

"Bad people?" asked Frog.

"Bad, too bad!" said Mama Frog. "Snakes are sneaks. They hide poison in their tongues, and they crush you in their coils."

Frogchild gulped.

"You be sure to hop out of Snake's reach if ever you meet again. And stop this slithering foolishness. Slithering's not for frogs."

Mama Frog set the table muttering to herself: "Playing with Snake! Now what is this, eh?" She rolled a steaming ball of gleaming cornmeal onto Frogchild's plate.

"Sit down and eat your funji, child," said Mama Frog. "And remember, I'm not fattening frogs for snakes, eh?"

Snake too reached home. He rustled the braided twig hatch-cover to his home. His mother knew his rustle and undid the vine latch. Snake toppled in.

"I'm hungry, Ma," he said, hopping all about.

"Eh, eh! Do good bless you! What a sight you are!" said Mama Snake. "Just look at you. And listen to your panting and wheezing. Where have you been all day?"

"In the bush, Mama, with my new friend. We played games. See what he taught me."

Snakeson jumped up on top of the table and leaped into the air. He came down on a stool, knocking it over and entangling himself in its legs.

"Eh, eh! Do good bless you. What a dangerous game that is," said Mama Snake. "Keep it up and see if you don't break every bone in your back. What new friend taught you that?"

She bent over and untangled her son from the stool.

"My frog friend taught me that. His name's Frogchild. It's the Frog-Hop Mama. Try it. It's fun."

"Frog, child?" Mama Snake's jaws hung open showing her fangs. "Did you say Frog, child?"

"Yes," said Snakeson. "He's my best friend."

"You mean you played all day with a frog and you come home hungry?"

"He was hungry too, Mama, after playing the Snake Slither game that I taught him."

"Eh, eh! Well do good bless you! Come, curl up here son and listen carefully to what I have to tell you."

Snakeson curled up on the stool.

"Don't you know, son, that it is the custom of our house to eat frogs? Frogs are delicious people!"

Snakeson's small eyes widened.

"Ah, for true!" said Mama Snake. "Eating frogs is the custom of our house, a tradition in our family. Hopping isn't, so cut it out, you hear me?"

"Oh, Mama," cried Snakeson. "I can't eat frogs. Frog's a friend."

"Frog a friend! Do good bless you!" said Mama Snake. "That's not natural. Now you listen to me, baby. The next time you play with Frog, jump roll and romp all you like. But when you get hungry, his game is up. Catch him and eat him!"

The next morning Snakeson was up early. He pushed off his dry-leaf cover and stretched himself. He remembered his mother's words, and the delicious feel of his frog friend when they had hugged. He was ready to go.

Mama Snake fixed her son a light breakfast of spiced insects and goldfinch eggs. Snakeson was soon on his way.

"Now don't you forget my instructions about frogs, do good bless you," Mama Snake called out after him. "And don't let me have to tell you again to watch out for big things with sharp claws and teeth that gnaw."

"Clawsangnaw," sang Snakeson. "Clawsangnaw."

He reached the bush and waited for his friend. He looked forward to fun with Frog, and he looked forward to finishing the fun with a feast of his fine frog friend. He lolled about in the sun, laughing and singing:

"You wish a wish
I'll wish a wish, too;
Can your wish and my wish
Both come true?"

The sun rose higher and higher, but Frog did not come.

"What's taking Frogchild so long," said Snakeson. "Perhaps too much slithering has given him the bellyache. I'll go and look for him."

Snake found Frog's rock home by the pond. He rolled up a stone in his tail and knocked on the rock door.

"Anybody home?"

"Just me," answered Frogchild.

"May I come in?"

"Ah, it's you Snakeson. Sorry, my Mama's out, and she said not to open the door to anyone."

"Come on out then and let's play," said Snakeson. "I waited all morning for you in the bush."

"I can't," said Frog, "not now, anyway."

"Oh, that's too bad," said Snake. "My mother taught me a new game. I'd love to teach it to you."

"I'll bet you would," said Frog.

"You don't know what you're missing," said Snake.

"But I do know what you're missing," said Frog, and he burst out laughing.

"Aha!" said Snake. "I see that your mother has given you instructions. My mother has given me instructions too."

Snake sighed. There was nothing more to say or do, so he slithered away.

Frog and Snake never forgot that day when they played together as friends. Neither ever again had that much fun with anybody.

Today you will see them, quiet and alone in the sun, still as stone. They are deep in thought remembering that day of games in the bush, and both of them wonder:

"What if we had just kept on playing together, and no one had ever said anything?"

But from that day to this, Frog and Snake have never played together again.

You wish a wish
I'll wish a wish, too;
May your wish and my wish
Both come true.

How Animals
Got Their Tails

I F YOU'RE TALKING about the beginning of things, you've got to go back, way, way back, back to the time when the animals had no tails.

That's right! In the beginning Raluvhimba, god of the Bavenda, created the animals without tails. Uh-huh! He never even gave tails a thought, uh-uh! not in the beginning.

When Raluvhimba came down from the heavens, he often sat in his favorite place on earth, high on Mount Tsha-wa-dinda. He'd relax there and admire the world that he had made: the mountains, rivers and trees, the sun, moon and stars.

"Uh-huh!" he'd say to himself, for in the beginning there was no one to uh-huh to. "Uh-huh! That sure looks good."

One day on Mount Tsha-wa-dinda, Raluvhimba lay down in Cave Luvhimbi and fell asleep. He dreamed a dream of animals that wandered the earth. And when he awoke, he set to work.

One by one Raluvhimba made the animals: Elephant and Mouse, Rabbit and Rhinoceros, Monkey and Ox, Lion and Fox. The large and the small, he made them all.

Raluvhimba worked hard to get each one right, Lion's first mane tripped him up, had to be shortened. Goats first coat was too tight a fit, had to be loosened. It took two tusks to complete Elephant, and it took a tusk or two to do Rhinoceros's snout.

Mouse was the last and the smallest of the creatures that Raluvhimba made.

"Uh-huh!" he said, holding Mouse in the palm of his hand. "How's that for small?"

"Uh-huh!" they all chanted back. "Small and beautiful."

But big or small, the animals had no color at all. So Raluvhimba mixed colors from the dye of plants. He took some
leftover bristles from Hog and made a brush. Then he painted
all the animals. Some he painted in plain colors, others he
daubed with spots, and on some he painted stripes.

"Now you're complete," he said. "Uh-huh! You sure look
good."

In those days no people were around. Raluvhimba hadn't yet thought of making man, so the animals had no one to fear. They roamed everywhere freely and fed on plants, shrubs and greens. They had good appetites, and they had good manners. They never even thought of eating each other. Uh-uh! Not in those days. They were vegetarians. The lion lay down with the lamb, and they all lived together peacefully.

Everywhere that Raluvhimba walked on earth there were animals to greet him. He was never without company on earth, and he liked that. But his trips through water and air were lonely; nobody in the water, nobody in the air.

Raluvhimba slept again in Cave Luvhimbi, and this time he dreamed of creatures for the water, creatures for the air.

He awoke and fleshed fish with scales to flash through the seas. He feathered birds for flight and tuned their voices to sing sweet songs.

"Uh-huh" cheered the animals. "That's some creating! It sure looks good!"

Now Raluvhimba had friends everywhere. Things couldn't have been better on earth, in the air or in the sea.

When he swam through the depths of the sea, the fish said "Lo!" as they saw him go. When he soared way up in the sky, the birds sang "Hi!" as he flew by. When he walked on earth, the animals said, "Pleasant day," as he passed their way, and they wiggled their ears for, as you remember, in those days the animals had no tails to waggle.

One day Raluvhimba played with the animals on Mount Tsha-wa-dinda. They liked seeing him make things so they circled him and chanted:

> *"O Creator create*
> *Make something new,*
> *Smaller than Mouse*
> *And alive, too."*

"Give it fine fur," said Fox.

"Mark it with stripes," said Zebra.

"Don't forget long ears," said Rabbit. "It will need long ears to wiggle."

Raluvhimba laughed. He closed his eyes and rubbed his forehead. An idea flickered. His fingers spun swiftly in space. Then he cupped his hands and blew into them. When he opened them, ahh! there stood Spider, alive and spinning.

"Oh, yeah! Now that is small," said Rabbit, "smaller than Mouse. No long ears, but he's sure got a lot of legs."

The animals crowded around and counted.

"One, two, three, four more than ours. Five, six more than birds. Seven, eight more than fish."

"Oh, eight legs, eight,
  And ain't none of them straight."

Spider spun a strand from Raluvhimba's fingers and dropped all the way down to the ground, *pim!* unhurt.

"Do it!" said the animals.

"Uh-huh!" said Spider, and he twirled back up the strand into Raluvhimba's hand.

"If you ever need a message delivered to the Master, call on me," said Spider. "I've got connections."

Spider's tie to Raluvhimba made him feel as important as Rabbit felt about his long ears. Raluvhimba was pleased that Spider was accepted by the animals as one of them. He decided to create more tiny creatures.

This time Raluvhimba made Fly and his mate, and they multiplied rapidly. And with insects came trouble.

At first flies fed on plant juice and dew as Spider did. But between meals they'd sit uninvited on the animals. Now Spider never did that; and even though Fly was light, the animals didn't like being sat on.

"Don't sit on me," said Rabbit.

"Go live on a tree," said Zebra.

"Take your big feet out of my mouth," said Ox.

62

So it went, day after day. One day when Fly was living high on the hog, he got fed up with all the complaints and took a bite out of Hog's hide. To his surprise he liked the taste. He bit again to make sure, then flew about tasting a few more hides.

"Umm, not bad," said Fly. "Tastier too than plant juice or dew."

Fly told a friend, "If you want a meal with body to it . . ." and word got around. Soon flies were tasting every animal in sight and sharing their best ideas for beast feasts.

"Try this," said Fly. "Taste Lion first, then take a bite of Deer, and finish with a nip of Rabbit. Dee-licious!"

The animals howled when bitten, they shook when tickled, they flinched when pinched. Suddenly one would leap up into the air, another would roll on the ground, another rub vigorously against a tree. Everyone knew why. The fault was Fly.

Finally the animals could stand it no longer. They called for Spider and asked if he would take a message to Raluvhimba.

"What's the message?" asked Spider.

63

"Flies are pests! Tell Raluvhimba that flies are not fit friends for animals. They're flesh-biters and blood-suckers. Tell him to take them back."

Spider didn't waste time. He tested a few strands and found one that led into the heavens.

"Aha, so it's you Spider," said Raluvhimba. "I thought I felt a tiny tug at my toe."

"Lo!" said Spider. He didn't waste time in greetings. "I've a message for you from the animals. They say flies are pests; they bite and they chew us, yes, that's what they do, and we don't want them around."

"What?" said Raluvhimba. "I can't take back what I've given. After all, that's life. Don't flies chew leaves for juice and suck dew as you do?"

"Oh, no, uh-uh, no!" said Spider. "Flies bite flesh and suck blood. That's the message. They're not fit friends for us. You've got to do something to help and fast. I play Free-the-Fly with them when they get caught in my web so I'm fine, but my friends are frantic."

Raluvhimba thought, "I can't believe that flies are a flaw in my creation."

But there it was, almost in the beginning. A small mistake uh-huh, a tiny one true, but a bad sign just the same, and man hadn't even been created yet.

"Listen Spider," said Raluvhimba, "instead of playing Free-the-Fly, suppose you ate the flies that stuck to your web?"

"Oo-oo," groaned Spider. The very idea made him sick. He was, after all, a vegetarian and had never even thought of eating fly meat.

"Stop groaning, Spider," said Raluvhimba. "I've a better idea. I'll make tails for animals to flick away the flies."

Spider sang:

> "Birds have tails
> Fish have tails
> The bird tail whishes
> The fish tail swishes.
> When's our day
> For tail's with which
> To flick and switch
> The flies away?"

"Today's Moon Day," said Raluvhimba. "Tell the animals I'll come down to Mount Tsha-wa-dinda tomorrow and make tails for all of them."

"Good," said Spider. "Today's Moon Day. Tomorrow's Choose Day. Choose Day's Tails Day."

Spider descended quickly and spread the word. When the animals heard the good news, they couldn't wait to choose a tail. They set out at once for Mount Tsha-wa-dinda. Only Rabbit, who was very lazy, went back to sleep.

"Get going, Long Ears," said Spider. "I know you heard the message."

"I don't see you going anywhere either," said Rabbit.

"I don't need a tail, but you do," said Spider.

"What's the rush?" said Rabbit. "There's lots of time, and there'll be lots of tails."

"Uh-huh," said Spider.

Rabbit yawned and fell asleep.

The next day Rabbit awoke to see animals passing by his burrow, wearing the most wonderful tails. Whenever a fly tried to land on an animal, it would swing its tail swoosh, swish, flick, and the fly would take off.

Animals with tails! A new scene on earth. Rabbit had to admit that it sure looked good. But even after his long rest, Rabbit was too lazy to stir himself.

"Who can I get to go for me," he thought. Then he saw Fox coming.

"Ah, Brother Fox," he said, "your tail is fantastic! Flies can't touch you now. I bet you run faster with it than you ever did before without it."

"Yeah!" said Fox. "This tail-piece does it. I'm fast now. I'm really fast."

"Brother Fox," said Rabbit, "since you're so much faster than I, would you run back and choose a fine tail for me?"

"Why sure, Brother Rabbit," said Fox, "be happy to do you the favor."

Fox sprang off, but he stopped to match tails with every animal he met along the way. It took him twice as long as it would have taken Rabbit to get there.

When Fox climbed up to Cave Luvhimbi, all the animals except Rabbit had already been there. He looked around and didn't see any tails at all. But as he turned to go, he spotted a short fur piece caught in the crevice of a rock.

"How stubby!" said Fox. "Can't flick flies much with that, but it's the only one left. Well, a long tail goes well with my short ears, so maybe a short tail will go well with long ears."

Fox took the tail and started back.

From his web in the high tree branches, Spider saw Fox approaching. He could make out only one bushy tail waving as Fox came closer. Spider said nothing of this when he dropped down beside Rabbit.

"Where's your tail?" asked Spider.

"Don't worry," said Rabbit. "It's coming."

Fox arrived and dropped the small fur ball before Rabbit.

"Here's your tail, Brother Rabbit," said Fox. "Not much of a tail, but it's all that was left. Still it is a tail, and that's the style nowadays."

Rabbit blinked his eyes.

"Here," said Fox, "let me help you put it on."

Rabbit was too stunned to move. Fox flipped him across his knees and tapped the tail into place. That done, Fox didn't wait around for thanks. He winked at Spider and ran off, laughing as he went.

Spider twirled back up to his web and sang under his breath:

*"Tails with which
to flick and switch
The flies away."*

Then he sang out loud and clear for Rabbit to hear:

"If you want a thing well done,
go do it yourself. Uh-huh, uh-huh!"

But Spider's moral only made Rabbit madder.

"That Fox, that sly Fox!" he cried. "What took him so long, huh? That's why I came out on the short end of it. I'll get even with him!"

But that tale leads to other tales of Rabbit and Fox, and here's where this tale ends. For whether it's an animal's tail or a told tale, be it long or short, whatever the sort, all must come to an end.

Uh-huh!